Dearest Anamik

Happy birthday!

Hope you enjoy this classic
picture book & poem about
the year and all seasons...
and know that you are
thought of and loved all
through the year, in
each & every season!

- Ramya chitti &
  Shiv chittappa

Jan 2007

JANUARY
Brings the Snow

By Sara Coleridge
Illustrated by Normand Chartier

🐿 A LITTLE SIMON BOOK
Published by Simon & Schuster, Inc., New York

For Heather, Andy, Casey, Mary-Beth, Andrew and Angel

JANUARY brings the snow,
Makes our feet and fingers glow.

FEBRUARY brings the rain,
Thaws the frozen lake again.

MARCH brings breezes, loud and shrill,
To stir the dancing daffodil.

APRIL brings the primrose sweet,
Scatters daisies at our feet.

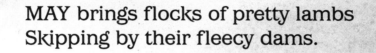

MAY brings flocks of pretty lambs
Skipping by their fleecy dams.

JUNE brings tulips, lilies, roses,
Fills the children's hands with posies.

Hot JULY brings cooling showers,
Apricots and gillyflowers.

AUGUST brings the sheaves of corn,
Then the harvest home is borne.

Warm SEPTEMBER brings the fruit;
Sportsmen then begin to shoot.

Fresh OCTOBER brings the pheasant;
Then to gather nuts is pleasant.

Dull NOVEMBER brings the blast;
Then the leaves are whirling fast.

Chill DECEMBER brings the sleet,
Blazing fire, and Christmas treat.